EARLY ONE MORNING AT HIGHER FOR HIRE---
FASTER THAN A SPEEDING AIRSHIP--
--MORE POWERFUL THAN A TURBINE--
--ABLE TO LEAP CITY BLOCKS IN A SINGLE BOUND--
--IT'S--
HIGHER FOR HIRE
KJB009-1

--DANGER WOMAN!!
AHHH--NUTHIN' ON THE SCHEDULE TODAY BUT R&R! AND, OH BOY, DO I LOOOOVE R&R!

WHAT'S R&R?

BALOO'S TWO FAVORITE LETTERS IN THE ALPHABET--
--RIGHT, POPPA BEAR?

HEH-HEH! Y'GOT THAT RIGHT, LI'L BRITCHES!
OKAY, EVERYONE, I NEED YOUR HONEST OPINIONS!

HOW DO I LOOK?

MOMMY! YOU'RE SO PRETTY!
WOW, MIZ CUNNINGHAM-- YOU LOOK GREAT!

WELL, BALOO? I DON'T HEAR YOU OFFERING A COMMENT!
SO--WHERE'RE YOUR CASTANETS?
HMPH!

WILL EVERYBODY BE DRESSED LIKE THAT ON THE BOAT, MOMMY?
I DON'T KNOW, SWEETIE! I'VE NEVER BEEN ON A DAY CRUISE BEFORE!
BUT I'VE HEARD THEY'RE LIKE BIG FLOATING PARTIES!

SOUNDS LIKE FUN!
SOUNDS STUPID, IF YA ASK ME!
C'MON, BECKY! IF YA WANT TO MEET NICE GUYS, GO TO LOUIE'S! MEET A REAL MAN-- NOT SOME RICH SNOB IN A FANCY-SCHMANCY SUIT WHO CALLS HIMSELF SKIPPY OR BIFFY OR--

WHY, BALOO-- ARE YOU JEALOUS?
JEALOUS? NOW WHY WOULD I BE JEALOUS?
OH, NO REASON! NEVER MIND!

COME ON, KIT-- I'LL GIVE YOU A RIDE!
NOW YOU WATCH OUT FOR SNAKES, LI'L BRITCHES--AN' POISON IVY!
GEE WHIZ, BALOO! I'M JUST GOIN' ON A HIKE WITH SOME KIDS FROM SCHOOL!

AND YOU'D BETTER TAKE GOOD CARE OF MOLLY, BUSTER! I DON'T WANT ANY TROUBLE!
RELAAAX! SHE'S GONNA BE GLUED TO THAT RADIO-- THEY'RE PLAYIN' A DANGER WOMAN MARATHON ALL DAY TODAY!

GOOD! THEN I'LL SEE YOU TONIGHT!
REMEMBER--NO TROUBLE, BALOO! I MEAN IT!
ALL RIGHT, ALREADY! I GET THE MESSAGE!
G'BYE, POPPA BEAR!

ME--JEALOUS! HA! THAT'S A GOOD ONE!
OH BOY OH BOY OH BOY--DANGER WOMAN ALL DAY LONG!
FWUMP!

AND DON'T FORGET, KIDS-- TODAY IS SATURDAY, DANGER WOMAN'S FAVORITE DAY! WHY?
BECAUSE EVERY SATURDAY, CAPE SUZETTE GETS A FRESH SUPPLY OF FROSTY PEP ICE CREAM! TELL YOUR MOM TO BUY YOU FROSTY PEP--DANGER WOMAN'S FAVORITE FOOD!

HOOOF!
BALOO, YOU'LL BUY ME SOME FROSTY PEP ICE CREAM TODAY, WON'T YOU, HUH? PLEASE OH PLEASE OH PLEEEEASE??
WOMP!

R&R...
I THINK IT'S GONNA STAND FOR RUN RAGGED!

DISNEY'S TALESPIN
FREEZE A JOLLY GOOD FELLOW!
MEANWHILE, FAR AWAY ON PIRATE ISLAND...
HAPPY BIRTHDAY TO ME! I'M AS YOUNG AS CAN BE! IF I NEVER HIT THIRTEEEE-- IT WILL NEVER HIT ME!

OOOH, DON KARNAGE, YOU HANDSOME RASCAL YOU! YOU HAVE NOT AGED ANY DAYS IN YEARS!
THERE IS NOTHING TO DO BUT ADMIT THE IMPLORABLE TRUTH-- YOU HAVE BEEN STAYING TWENTY-NINE FOREVER, HEE HEEEE!

=GASP!= I ALMOST FORGOT!

CLICK!
STOP, CANOLLI! I'VE CAUGHT YOU RED-HANDED!
DON'T COUNT ON IT, DANGER WOMAN! ROCKO AND I HAVE WAYS OF DEALING WITH YOU!
OH, PHOOEY! I MISSED THE BEGINNING!

KNOCK! KNOCK!
IF YOU BROUGHT A PRESENT FOR THE BIRTHDAY BOY, COME IN!
AND NOW A WORD FROM OUR SPONSOR--

UH... HAPPY BIRTHDAY, CAP'N!
GRAZIE, GRAZIE! NOW WHAT IS YOUR MATTER?
WELL, IT'S ABOUT YOUR PARTY TONIGHT! I-I MEAN, YOUR SURPRISE PARTY TONIGHT...

WHAT ABOUT MY SURPRISE PARTY TONIGHT? IS THERE SOMETHING WRONG ABOUT MY SURPRISE PARTY TONIGHT?
NO, NO! IT'S JUST, WELL...

...WE'VE BEEN ABLE TO GET EVERYTHING ON YOUR LIST BUT THESE TWO ITEMS!
THE CAKE AND ICE CREAM?!
HOW CAN I HAVE A BIRTHDAY PARTY WITHOUT CAKE AND ICE CREAM?!
WE'VE CAPTURED SIX PLANES SO FAR THIS MORNING, CAP'N, BUT NOBODY'S CARRYING PARTY SUPPLIES! WHAT'RE WE SUPPOSED TO--?

WAIT-- LISTEN!
FWAK!
AND DON'T FORGET, KIDS-- TODAY IS SATURDAY, DANGER WOMAN'S FAVORITE DAY! WHY?

BECAUSE EVERY SATURDAY CAPE SUZETTE GETS A FRESH SUPPLY OF FROSTY PEP ICE CREAM!
AH-HA AND DOUBLE AH-HA!!

YOU HAVE SO LITTLE FAITH, MY ESTUPID STOOGE! HAVE YOU NEVER HEARD OF THE GREAT BIRTHDAY RULE?
WHAT A BIRTHDAY BOY WANTS--
--A BIRTHDAY BOY GETS!

AND SO, LATER THAT MORNING...
BUT, DANGER WOMAN--IT COULD BE A TRAP!
OF COURSE IT'S A TRAP, COMMISSIONER! THAT'S WHY I HAVE TO GO IN!
THEN BE CAREFUL, DANGER WOMAN!

WE INTERRUPT THIS PROGRAM FOR A SPECIAL NEWS BULLETIN!
THE CARGO PLANE CARRYING THIS WEEK'S SHIPMENT OF "FROSTY PEP" ICE CREAM HAS BEEN HIJACKED! STAY TUNED FOR DETAILS AS THEY DEVELOP!
GASP!

BALOO! BALOO, WAKE UP! IT'S BEEN STOLEN!
W-WHO--??
WHERE--??!
WHAT'S BEEN STOLEN?!

THE FROSTY PEP ICE CREAM PLANE! SOMEBODY TOOK IT! THE RADIO JUST SAID SO!

ICE CREAM? AW, BUTTON NOSE, THE POLICE'LL HANDLE IT! WE CAN'T DO ANYTHING!
BUT... BUT HOW CAN YOU GET ME SOME FROSTY PEP IF THERE ISN'T ANY?
I GUESS YOU'LL HAVE TO TAKE A RAIN CHECK. I'M SORRY.

CAN'T WE GO LOOK FOR IT? OH PLEASE, BALOO?
Y'MEAN IN THE SEA DUCK? I DON'T THINK WE...
...NOW, MOLLY, DON'T LOOK AT ME LIKE THAT-- I--I...

PLEEEEEEASE?

AWW, MAN, THIS KID'S GOOD!
SHE'S REEEEAL GOOD!

MEANWHILE...
SAY YOUR PRAYERS, DANGER WOMAN! YOU'VE INTERRUPTED MY PLANS FOR THE LAST TIME!
BLAST HER, ROCKO!
FROSTY PEP
FP
BUT, BOSS-- LOOK UP!
A NET-- IT'S COMING DOWN ON US! AAAARGH!!

NICE TRY, CANOLLI, BUT YOU AND YOUR GANG ARE THE CATCH OF THE DAY!
HEE HEE-- OOOOH, I JUST LOVE IT WHEN SHE TINFOILS THE BAD GUYS!
OH, CAPTAIN!

WHAT WHAT WHAT?!
VAT DO YOU VANT US TO DO VIT DEES TWO? DA USUAL?

YOU KNOW, I AM FEELING STRANGELY MAGNAMONEOUS TODAY!
I THINK WE SHALL GIVE THEM ONE PARACHUTE TO SHARE BETWEEN EACH OTHER--
--THEN PUSH THEM OUT!

HSSSSP SPSSSP HSSSSP!
A BAND? WHAT--A RUBBER BAND? WHAT ARE YOU TALKING ABOUT??
FROSTY PEP

HE MEANS FOR TONIGHT, CAP'N! Y'KNOW-- MUSIC!
OH! THAT IS A VERY GOOD IDEA, YES!
I WAS JUST ABOUT TO THINK OF IT MYSELF!

I PUT YOU IN CHARGE OF FINDING ONE!
M-ME?? WHERE DO I LOOK?!
MUST I TELL YOU EVERYTHING? JUST FIND ONE AND BRING IT BACK!
OR ELSE!

NOW, THAT LEAVES NOTHING NOT GOTTEN BUT THE CAKE!
HMMM...WHERE CAN I GET A GREAT BIG CAKE?

GRAB!
HSSP SPSSP SSPSP!

SNITCH!
WHAT DO YOU MEAN, FROM A GREAT BIG BAKERY, YOU--

UNO MENUDO--THAT IS IT! I KNOW WHERE TO GET THE PERFECT CAKE FOR MY PARTY!
WAIT--YOU'RE DOING ALL THIS FOR A PARTY?! YOU'RE CRAZY, KARNAGE!

I AM NOT CRAZY!
I AM JUST ONE HECK OF A FUN-FALUTING GUY, HEE HEE!
BAP!
BOOT!

HAPPY LANDINGS, GENTLEMEN!
IT'S MINE!
NO, IT'S MINE!!

FIRST I MUST TAKE THE BOOTY HOME BEFORE IT MELTS!
THEN I SHALL RUN A SPECIAL ERRAND!

LATER, ELSEWHERE OVER THE OCEAN...
I DON'T SEE THE FROSTY PEP PLANE ANYWHERE, TRUSTY SIDEKICK!
ME NEITHER, MOLLY--ER, I MEAN, DANGER WOMAN!

BALOO, WHAT IF WE DON'T FIND IT? WHAT IF IT'S GONE AND THERE'S NO MORE FROSTY PEP ICE CREAM EVER AGAIN?!
I GOT IT! HOW 'BOUT WE GO TO LOUIE'S? IF ANYBODY'D KNOW WHERE TO LOOK FOR ICE CREAM, OL' LOUIE WOULD!
SNAP!

AN' WHILE WE'RE THERE, YOU CAN HAVE A BIG KRAKATOA SPECIAL TO CHEER YA UP, OKAY?
OH, BOY!

UM, I MEAN--GOOD IDEA, TRUSTY SIDEKICK! PUT THE DANGER PLANE IN SUPER-DOOPER HIGH GEAR AND SET A COURSE FOR LOUIE'S PLACE!
AYE-AYE, CAPTAIN DANGER WOMAN, MA'AM-SIR!

MEANWHILE, ABOARD THE SS FESTIVIA...
HOOHAH!
YIP YIP!
WHOOPEE!
HA HA!
WHEEEE!

THANK YOU, THANK YOU!
CONGA LINES ARE MY SPECIALTY!

AND HOW ARE YOU AT SLOW DANCING, MISS...?
PLEASE CALL ME REBECCA. AND...LET ME GUESS... YOUR NAME IS SKIPPY?
HEAVENS NO! MY NAME IS JOHN!
BUT CALL ME TADDY! EVERYBODY DOES!

SO, REBECCA--WHAT DO YOU SAY WE GO ASK THE BAND TO PLAY "MOONLIGHT MELODY," SHALL WE?
SURE--WHY NOT?

WHILE, NOT FAR AWAY...
THIS IS JUST DANDY! GIBBER COMES UP WITH SOME FANCY-PANTS IDEA, AN' WE DO ALL THE WORK!
AN' IF WE COME BACK EMPTY-HANDED, THE CAPTAIN'LL STRING US UP BY OUR EARLOBES!
OH, QUIT YOUR WHINING AND KEEP LOOKING!

HOT DOG--JACKPOT AT SIX O'CLOCK!!

"MOONLIGHT MELODY"? WHY, IT JUST SO HAPPENS THAT'S THE VERY NEXT SONG WE'RE GOING TO PLAY, BEAUTIFUL!
THANK YOU!

THOONK
THONK
LOOK--
--AIR PIRATES!!
FWOCK
THOONK!

HELLLLP!!
JUMP, REBECCA-- I'LL CATCH YOU!

WAIT, WHAT AM I SAYING??
I'D RUIN MY SUIT!

AIIIIEEEEE!
CATCH THIS!!

HOLD ON, MISS! WE'VE GOT YOU!
HURRY! I'M SLIPPING!!

OHHH-- PANT PANT THANK YOU!
ANY TIME!
OMIGOSH-- WE'RE BEING KIDNAPPED!

BUT WHAT WOULD AIR PIRATES WANT US FOR?
SOON, AT LOUIE'S PLACE...
BALOO, DIG THESE FIRE-CRACKERS! I'M CATERING A BIG SHINDIG TONIGHT ON PAIR-O'-DICE ISLAND!
THAT FLOATING CASINO PLACE?
YOU GOT IT! DINNER, DANCING, THE WHOLE SHEBANG--EVEN A FIREWORKS DISPLAY! MAN, IT'S GONNA BE SOME WILD PARTY!

SO WHAT BRINGS YOU TO MY PLACE, YOUNG-SHORT-AND-GORGEOUS?
TEE HEE-- ICE CREAM! BALOO SAID YOU'D MAKE ME A CRACK-YOUR-TOE SPECIAL!

I DON'T HAVE ANY ICE CREAM, CUZ! MY SHIPMENT DIDN'T COME THIS MORNING!
AW, GREAT-- I DIDN'T KNOW YOU WERE SUPPLIED BY THE SAME CARGO RUN AS CAPE SUZETTE!
NO ICE CREAM, BALOO?

DON'T YOU FRET, CUTIE PIE! I'LL GET YOU THE NEXT BEST THING--
--LOUIE'S PILE-TO-THE-SKY FRUIT DELIGHT! WITH WHIPPED CREAM AND A CHERRY ON TOP!
OKAY!

FELICITATIONAL GREETINGS, ONE AND EVERYBODY!
IT IS I, THE PIRATE OF THE HOUR-- DON KARNAGE!

NOW NOW, GENTLEMEN-- I HAVE NOT A WEAPON IN MY HANDS, LOOK-SEE?
WHAT'RE YOU DOING HERE, KARNAGE?
I COME TO BUY A ROUND OF YOUR MOST TASTY DRINKS FOR ALL THESE THIRSTY PATRON-TYPES!

HUH??

RIGHT--AND I SELL PROPELLERS DOOR-TO-DOOR! NOW WHAT ARE YOU REALLY AFTER, KARNY?
FOR THE UMPTIMILLIONTH TIME, BALOO, MY NAME IS KARNAGE--DON KARNAGE! AND I AM AFTER NOTHING TODAY BUT A BIRTHDAY--
--MINE!

YA DON'T SAY! SO JUST HOW MANY CANDLES WILL YOU BE PUTTIN' ON YOUR CAKE THIS YEAR, YOU OL' PIRATE YOU?
MY...
...CANDLES...
ARE NONE OF YOUR COTTON-PLUCKING FLOOR WAX, YOU SNOOPSY SIMIAN!
BUT, CAPTAIN--YOU SAID YOU VERE TVENTY-NINE YEARS OLD DIS MORNING!
BUT COME TO TINK OV IT, YOU SAID DAT LAST YEAR, TOO! AND DA YEAR BEFORE DAT! AND DA YEAR BE--
REMIND ME TO SHOOT YOU WHEN WE GET HOME!
ERR-- SORRY, CAPTAIN!
=AHEM!= NOW, LOUIE, I HAVE COME TO ORDER A CAKE FROM YOUR MOST ABLE BAKERY--
--A VERY LARGE ICE CREAM CAKE--WITH LOTS OF CHOCOLATE FROSTING AND THE LITTLE SPRINKLY DOOHICKIES ON TOP!
NO CAN DO, KARNAGE! EVEN IF I HAD THE TIME--AND THE INCLINATION--I DON'T HAVE THE ICE CREAM!
OH, THAT IS NO PROBLEM--I BROUGHT MY OWN!
HEY, THAT'S THE STOLEN FROSTY PEP!!

OF COURSE IT IS!
I STOLE IT!
WHY, YOU--
CHINK!
CHINK!
BUT I WILL PAY FOR IT WHEN I PICK IT UP! WHAT DO YOU THINK OF THAT?
SINCE WHEN DID YOU EVER PAY FOR ANYTHING, KARNAGE?

WHAT THAT GUY NEEDS IS A GOOD BIRTHDAY SPANKIN'!
Y'KNOW, HE DIDN'T JUST STEAL THE FROSTY PEP--HE TOOK THE WHOLE DARN PLANE! THOSE PILOTS CAN'T WORK WITHOUT THEIR PLANE!
AN' NOW THIS!

I HATE THIS! WHAT IF KARNAGE DISCOVERS I'M A PHONY?
HAPPY BERTHDAY CAP'N KARNAGE!
HE WON'T! NOW DON'T WORRY, MA'AM-- WE'LL GET OUT OF THIS MESS SOMEHOW!
DON'T WORRY? EASY FOR YOU TO SAY! THAT PIRATE RAT ISN'T LEERING AT YOU!

MAD DOG, MY NORMALLY DIMWITTED FLUNKY-- I AM PROUD OF YOU!
NOT ONLY DID YOU GO OUT AND FIND A BAND, BUT YOU FOUND A GOOD ONE! WITH A MOST INTRIGUING DANCER...
GEE-- THANKS, CAP'N!

IN FACT, GO FETCH HER HERE TO ME!

WHEN'RE YOU GONNA OPEN YOUR PRESENTS, CAPTAIN? 'SPECIALLY THAT BIG ONE! I'M SURPRISED LOUIE GAVE IT TO YOU, CONSIDERIN' YOU STIFFED HIM FOR THE CAKE AN' SUNDAES!
RATTLE!
RATTLE!
HAPPY BIRTHDAY KARNAGE Louie
HOW MANY TIMES MUST I TELL YOU, HACKSAW-- YOUR CAPTAIN IS ADORED BY ALL-- EVEN HIS ENEMIES!

MEANWHILE, IN THE KITCHEN...
EVERY YEAR IT'S THE SAME THING--TWENTY-NINE CANDLES!
TALK ABOUT GETTIN' STUCK IN A RUT!

I C-CAN'T **BELIEVE** LOUIE T-T-TALKED ME **INTO** THIS! I'M F-F-**FREEZIN'** IN HERE!
DANGER WOMAN DOESN'T **GET** COLD!
SO WHEN DO WE **JUMP OUT** AND **ATTACK** THE PIRATES?

WE'RE N-**NOT** GONNA AT-T-TACK **ANYBODY!** YOU KNOW THE PLAN--**WAIT** T-TILL IT'S QUIET, **SNEAK** OUT, **LIGHT** THOSE C-CANDLES--AN' THEN R-**RUN!**
AND WE'LL **RESCUE** THE FROSTY PEP PLANE, **TOO?**
W-WE **HAVE** TO--IT'S OUR T-T-TICKET **OUTTA** HERE!

SO, WHAT IS YOUR **NAME,** MY PRANCING PIGEON?
NONE OF YOUR **BUSINESS!**
GEE, **THAT'S** A WEIRD NAME!

IT'S T-TOO DOGGONE **C-C-COLD** IN HERE!
I-I THINK I'M GONNA S-**SNEEZE!** AHHH--
BALOO, YOU **CAN'T** SNEEZE-- SOMEBODY'S **OUT** THERE!
--AHH-- **AHHHH--**
WHERE DO YOU THINK **YOU** ARE GOING, LOVELY ONE? YOU MUST **STAY** WITH ME FOR THE **GRAND FINALITY!**

FOR HE'S A JOLLY GOOD PIRATE!
FOR HE'S A JOLLY GOOD PIRATE!
FOR HE'S A JOLLY GOOD
PIIIIIRAAAAATE--
THAT NOBODY DARES DEFY!!!
--AHHH--
AHHHH--
WHONK!
FWIP!
SURPRISE!
AACHOOO!
FOOOSH!
OOPS.

BALOO?!?

BALOO!?!

MOMMY!!

BECKY?!?

BECKY??

MOLLY?!
GET THEM!

HERE, FELLAS-- HAVE SOME CAKE!
SPLORT!

C'MON, BECKERS-- PARTY'S OVER!
WHAT IN THE-- ?!?
HEY! WAIT FOR US!

BALOO, WHAT ARE YOU DOING HERE WITH MY DAUGHTER?!
WHAT WERE YOU DOIN' HOLDIN' KARNY'S HAND?!
I WAS KIDNAPPED, YOU MORON! AND I WASN'T HOLDING HIS HAND--HE WAS HOLDING MINE!
THEN WHO ARE THESE GUYS?
WE'RE THE BAND FROM THE CRUISE! WE WERE KIDNAPPED, TOO!
REALLY? BALOO AND ME CAME HERE ON PURPOSE!
ON PURPOSE?! BALOO, WHAT--
OH MY GOODNESS...
MAN OH MAN, I THINK WE HIT THE HEART OF PIRATE CENTRAL!!
MOMMY, LOOK AT ALL THE MONEY! THE PIRATES ARE RICH!
THIS ISN'T THEIR MONEY, SWEETIE-- THEY TOOK IT FROM PEOPLE LIKE YOU AND ME!
YEAH-- AN' WE'RE GONNA TAKE SOME BACK!
BALOO, YOU CAN'T BE SERIOUS! THAT'S STEALING!
LOOK, KARNY OWES A COUPLA DEBTS!
I'M JUST GONNA MAKE SURE HE PAYS UP!
HERE!!
THIS OUGHTTA COVER YOUR TIME AND TROUBLE!
WOW-- WILL IT EVER!

THIS WAY!
BALOO, THEY'RE COMING!
JUST A SECOND! KARNY OWES LOUIE AN' THOSE FROSTY PEP PILOTS, TOO!
BUT THERE'S NO TIME!

BET DANGER WOMAN CAN MAKE SOME!
?!

THEY'RE IN THE TREASURY-- TRYING TO STEAL OUR STOLEN STUFF!
HURRY!

HEY--PUT THOSE BACK!
Y'WANT 'EM? COME AN' GET 'EM!

FIRE!!
PONK!
BINK!
BIP!
YIIEEEE! WHOA! WHOOOPS!
AS MY DEAR OL' MOM USED T'SAY--

--WHEN YOU'RE IN A RUSH, JUST SWEEP THE DIRT UNDER THE CARPET!
HEY! WHO TURNED OUT THE LIGHTS??
DO YOU HAVE ANY IDEA WHERE WE'RE GOING, BALOO?
SURE I DO--THE DOCKING BAY! IT SHOULD BE RIGHT AROUND THIS CORNER--
OKAY, MAYBE I NEED A MAP!
YOU WILL NEED MORE THAN A MAP WHEN I AM THROUGH WITH YOU, YOU UNINVITED PARTY CRASHER!
RUN FOR IT!!
DO NOT LET THEM GET AWAY, MEN!
SHOOT TO STOP!!
BALOO, LOOK UP AHEAD--WE'RE TRAPPED!
"NO NEED TO FEAR WITH DANGER WOMAN NEAR!"
LOOK, EVERYBODY--A DANGER-MOBILE!
GANGWAY!!
NOOOO!
BLAM!

AFTER THEM... MEN...
URGHHH
OOOOH
UHHHHH

SLOW DOWN, BALOO!
WITH WHAT? I CAN'T EVEN STEER!!
WHEEE-EEEEE!

OOOF!
WHAM!
WELL, AT LEAST WE LANDED ON SOMETHING SOFT!
AN' WE'RE BACK AT THE PARTY! THIS IS GREAT!
GREAT?! WE'RE BACK WHERE WE STARTED FROM!
BUT NOW I CAN GIVE KARNAGE HIS PRESENT!
YOU'RE GIVING THAT SLIMY PIRATE A BIRTHDAY PRESENT?!?
NOPE!
BUT LOUIE IS!
THEY JUST UP AN' DIS-APPEARED, CAP'N!
NOBODY UPS AND DISAPPEARS FROM DON KARNAGE! WE WILL SPLIT UP AGAIN AND--
OH, KARNEEEE! WE'RE DOWN HEEEEEERE!

NOW WE MAKE OUR GET-AWAY!
BUT THIS IS THE WRONG DOOR!
NO, THIS IS THE RIGHT DOOR, MOMMY! HE TOOK THE WRONG DOOR LAST TIME!
SO WHERE'D THEY GO?
AND WHO LIT ALL THE LITTLE BIRTHDAY FUSES?
FUSES?!
BANG!
POP!
BAM!
BLOOOIE!
IS IT OVER... ??
THAT WAS IT? A FEW LITTLE BOOM-BOOMS IN THE ICE CREAM?
THAT BALOO, HE IS ONE VERY ESTRANGE FELLOW!
SSSSSSS
LOOK OUT--THAT ONE HASN'T GONE OFF YET!
SO? I WILL JUST PUT OUT THE LITTLE FLAME!
NO FLAME, NO BOOM-BOOM, YES-NO?

SSSSSSSS
UH-OH.
HAPPY BIRTHDAY KARNAGE Louie
RUMBLE RUMBLE

EVERY-BODY IN-- PRONTO! WE'RE TAKIN' OFF!
BALOO, I DON'T KNOW HOW YOU DID IT, BUT YOU SAVED US!
AND THE FROSTY PEP!
WELL, HANG ON--WE'RE NOT OUTTA THIS YET!
WHY, WHAT'S WRONG? WHAT'S IN THAT BIG BOX THAT LOUIE GAVE KARNAGE, ANYWAY?
HEE HEE-- YOU'LL SEE, MOMMY!
FROSTY PEP
OH...YES, I DO SEE! I SEE VERY WELL!
HEH HEH! WE GAVE OL' KARNY WHAT HE WANTED MOST OF ALL--
--A REAL BANG-UP OF A BIRTHDAY PARTY!!

Disney's TaleSpin
Contractual Desperation!
HIGHER FOR HIRE
ONE AFTERNOON, AT "HIGHER FOR HIRE"...
YIPPEEE! WE DID IT!
WE DID IT! WE DID IT!
KJB005
KIT-- I AM THE HAPPIEST BUSINESSWOMAN IN THE WHOLE WORLD!
WE FINALLY PUT HIGHER FOR HIRE BACK IN THE BLACK!
THE BLACK-- ??
A BUSINESS TERM, KIT! IT MEANS THAT HIGHER FOR HIRE IS OUT OF DEBT!
FLICK!
WOW, MIZ CUNNINGHAM-- THAT'S GREAT!

WHIRRRRRRR!
KRASH!
Waaaahh!!
SO--WHILE I WAS OUT PAYING CREDITORS, HOW DID THINGS GO HERE IN THE OFFICE?

NOTHING BUT SMOOTH FLYING SINCE YOU LEFT THIS MORN-ING!
HERE ARE YOUR PHONE MESSAGES!

MY, YOU'RE SO ORGANIZED! THANK YOU FOR COVERING THE PHONES INSTEAD OF BALOO!
WHENEVER HE DEALS WITH CLIENTS, SOMETHING ALWAYS GOES WRONG!

BY THE WAY-- WHERE IS BALOO? I DID LEAVE HIM OFFICIALLY IN CHARGE.
OH, HE, UH, WENT TO GET A BURGER! BUT, WELL...
...HE SHOULD HAVE BEEN BACK AN HOUR AGO...

YOU DON'T HAVE TO COVER FOR HIM, KIT! I HATE TO SAY IT, BUT I'M RATHER RELIEVED THAT HE ISN'T HERE!
AFTER ALL, HE CAN'T GET INTO TROUBLE BUY-ING A HAMBURGER! THAT'S ONE THING HE KNOWS HOW TO DO RIGHT!

WHEN HE COMES BACK, TELL HIM I WANT TO SEE HIM!
WILL DO, MIZ CUNNINGHAM!

THERE, YOU ARE, POPPA BEAR! WHERE'VE YOU BEEN? MIZ CUNNINGHAM WANTS TO SEE YOU!
PT-PT-RRRMMMMM!

NOW, THAT'S WHAT I CALL A COINCIDENCE, 'CAUSE I WANT TO SEE BECKY!
UH-OH-- I'VE HEARD THAT TONE OF VOICE BEFORE! WHAT ARE YOU UP TO?
HEH-HEH-- YOU KNOW ME TOO WELL, LI'L BRITCHES!

YEEEAAH--
--OH, HI, GUYS!
HI, WILDCAT!
NEERROOM!

I'VE BEEN THINKIN' ABOUT HOW WELL BECKY'S RUNNIN' THE BUSINESS! I MEAN, SHE'S BEEN DOIN' A BANG-UP JOB! SO, I DECIDED TO HELP OUT!
I BOOKED SOME EXTRA WORK TO GENERATE A LITTLE CASH FOR THE OL' COFFERS!

WAIT A SECOND-- YOU? BOOKED WORK?
EXTRA??
I JUST WANT BECKY TO KNOW I APPRECIATE HER HARD WORK, THAT'S ALL!

WAIT--YOU'RE TRYING TO BUTTER HER UP, AREN'T YOU?
YOU WANT A RAISE, RIGHT? OR A VACATION?
VRRROOOMMMMM!

KIT, I'M SURPRISED AT YOU! YOU THINK THE ONLY REASON I'D BE NICE TO HER IS TO GET A RAISE OR A VACATION?!
WELL... ER...

HECK, I GOT SOMETHIN' BETTER IN MIND!

SEE, I FIGURE IT THIS WAY--IF I BRING IN A FANCY CLIENT OR TWO ON MY OWN, BECKY'LL HAVE TO ADMIT THAT I GOT A NOODLE FOR BUSINESS, RIGHT?
MAYBE SHE'LL GIVE ME A SAY IN WHAT GOES ON AROUND HERE! MOVE ME UP INTO MANAGEMENT!
ZOOOOMM!

DON'T GET YOUR HOPES UP, BALOO.
HEY, IT'S A PIECE O' CAKE! I'M READY TO HANDLE MORE RESPONSIBILITY, AN' THIS'LL PROVE IT!
BESIDES, A PROMOTION WOULD MEAN AN AUTO-MATIC RAISE IN SALARY ANYWAY, RIGHT?
ZZOWWW
BASH!

Ahem!
AH, BALOO! GOOD! I WANT TO TALK TO YOU!
AN' I WANT TO TALK TO YOU! I'M GONNA NEED TO USE THE SEA DUCK A LITTLE EXTRA THIS WEEK AN'--

EXTRA? FOR WHAT EXTRA?
WHAT ARE YOU UP TO? WHERE ARE YOU PLANNING ON GOING? ARE YOU TRYING TO SNEAK ANOTHER VACATION?
HEH HEH! I JUST LOVE IT WHEN YOU JUMP TO CONCLUSIONS!
TAKE A A GANDER AT THIS!

A CONTRACT?
IT SAYS YOU'VE AGREED TO PICK UP CARGO FROM A WAREHOUSE ON THE ISLAND OF YIRJOSHINMEE FOR SOMEBODY NAMED T. BONE PICKER!
WHAT DOES THIS MEAN, BALOO?
JUST WHAT IT SAYS--I ARRANGED A LITTLE EXTRA WORK!

YOU?
EXTRA WORK?

HIGHER FOR HIRE'S DOIN' PRETTY GOOD THESE DAYS, AN' I JUST WANTED TO, WELL, DO SOME-THING FOR THE COMPANY!
WE'RE NOT SO BUSY THAT WE CAN'T FIT IN ONE MORE HIGH-PAYING CLIENT, ARE WE?

YOU'RE REALLY SERIOUS! YOU ACTUALLY DID THIS FOR THE COMPANY!
BALOO, THAT'S THE SWEETEST GESTURE--ESPECIALLY COMING FROM SOMEONE LIKE YOU!

AIN'T IT, THOUGH?

SHE'S GONNA CATCH ON TO YOU, BALOO! WHY DON'T YOU JUST BE HONEST AND TELL HER WHAT YOU WANT?
'CAUSE I GOTTA PROVE MYSELF FIRST! IT'S ONLY A MATTER O' TIME BEFORE BECKY RECOGNIZES MY TRUE POTENTIAL AN' THEN--

YIIIEEEEE!!

F-F-FINE PRINT! R-R-READ THE F-F-FINE PRINT!!
WHAT FINE PRINT??
"FAILURE TO FULFILL THIS CONTRACT BY 10:00 A.M. TOMORROW WILL RESULT IN THE FORFEITURE OF THE BUSINESS ENTITY KNOWN AS HIGHER FOR HIRE TO T. BONE PICKER."
AND SOMEWHERE IN DOWNTOWN CAPE SUZETTE...
GULP!
YOU SAY YOU FOUND THIS CLOWN IN A BURGER JOINT?
YEAH!
BALOO'S AIR SERVICE
HIGHER FOR HIRE

HE WAS TALKIN' ABOUT HOW HIS BUSINESS WAS GROWING AND HOW HE WANTED TO MAKE EXTRA MONEY FOR HIS BOSS!
HE'S JUST WHAT WE WAS LOOKIN' FOR, RIGHT?

OH, HE'S PERFECT, ALL RIGHT!
I DID SOME QUICK RESEARCH AND, AS YOU CAN SEE, HIGHER FOR HIRE HAS GROWN IN THE LAST YEAR--YET IT'S STILL SMALL ENOUGH FOR US TO HANDLE!
WE GOT US A PIGEON, BOYS!

RING!
RING!
HEH HEH--I BET HE'S FINALLY NOTICED THE FINE PRINT!

HELLOOO... ??

MOMENTS LATER...
THANK YOU SO MUCH, MR. PICKER! I'LL SEE YOU SHORTLY!

MR. PICKER IS COMING OVER HERE, BALOO. MAYBE I CAN STRAIGHTEN THIS MESS OUT.
IN THE MEANWHILE, I DON'T WANT YOU GOING ANYWHERE! DO YOU UNDERSTAND ME?
ULP! YES, BOSS.

AND SOON...
IT'S PERFECTLY IN ORDER, MIZ CUNNINGHAM. YOUR MR. BALOO SIGNED THIS CONTRACT AS ATTORNEY-IN-FACT OF HIGHER FOR HIRE!
ATTORNEY-IN-WHAT??

WILL YOU EXCUSE US FOR A MOMENT, PLEASE?

DESPITE THE FACT THAT I SHOULD HAVE KNOWN BETTER, I LEFT YOU IN CHARGE OF HIGHER FOR HIRE WHILE I WAS GONE, BALOO.
LEGALLY, YOUR SIGNATURE HAD THE POWER OF MY SIGNATURE DURING THAT TIME...

...BUT YOU WEREN'T SUPPOSED TO SIGN ANYTHING!!
GURK--!!

PLEASE, MIZ CUNNINGHAM, THERE'S NO NEED TO BE UPSET-- THIS CONTRACT IS SIMPLY MY WAY OF PROTECTING MY INTERESTS!
YOU SEE, IT'S VERY IMPORTANT THAT MY SHIPMENT ARRIVES BY 10:00 A.M. TOMORROW!

TIMELY DELIVERY IS THE ONLY THING THAT CONCERNS ME-- TRULY! I'M SURE YOUR PILOT WILL HAVE NO TROUBLE MAKING THE DEADLINE!
THERE IS ABSOLUTELY NOTHING FOR YOU TO WORRY ABOUT!

MEANWHILE, OUT ON THE DOCK...
NOW LET'S SEE... MAYBE IF I JUST TIGHTEN THIS AND READJUST THAT...

CHIR?
CHIR?
Shhh! NO CHIR! YOU'VE HAD ENOUGH!

BUT WHAT ABOUT THIS WIRE? HMM...
LET'S PULL IT OUT AN' SEE WHAT HAPPENS!

FZZT CRCKKL!
OUCH!!

OKAY, LET'S PUT IT BACK IN...

YIRJOSHINMEE'S NOT *THAT,* FAR, BECKY!
IF I LEAVE *SOON,* I'LL MAKE IT BACK IN *PLENTY O'* TIME!

YOU *IDIOT!* I'M NOT LETTING *ONE* UNNECESSARY SECOND GO BY! YOU'RE LEAVING *RIGHT NOW!* AND IF YOU'RE NOT BACK BEFORE *10 A.M.* TOMORROW-- *WITH* THE *CARGO*--SO HELP ME I'LL--

OKAY, OKAY! I DON'T NEED TO HEAR THE GORY *DETAILS!*
I'M *GOIN'* ALREADY!

WILDCAT, DID YOU FIX THE *ENGINE?*
UH-- *WHAT* ENGINE?
OH! THE *SEA DUCK* ENGINE THAT WAS MAKIN' THE FUNNY *NOISE?* UHHH...
...*NO.*

WILDCAT, IF I DON'T LEAVE FOR YIRJOSHINMEE *RIGHT NOW,* BECKY'LL SKIN ME *ALIVE!* NOW *WHY* DIDN'T YOU FIX THAT *ENGINE?!*
'CAUSE I'VE BEEN WORKIN' ON *THIS*--A *MOTORIZED PARACHUTE!* IT CAN'T TEAR OR COLLAPSE LIKE A *REGULAR* PARACHUTE!
NEAT *IDEA,* HUH?

SO *THAT'S* WHAT THIS THING IS!
YUP! MIZ CUNNINGHAM SAID SHE WANTS *HIGHER FOR HIRE* TO BE ON THE *CUTTING EDGE* OF TECHNOLOGY!

I THINK THIS IS PRETTY SHARP, DON'T *YOU?*

GREAT! *NOW* WHAT AM I GONNA *DO?!*
UM... GET *MAD* AT ME?

NAW--THAT'D TAKE TOO MUCH TIME! I THINK I'LL TAKE YOU WITH ME INSTEAD!
THEN IF SOME-THIN' GOES HAYWIRE, YOU'LL BE THERE TO FIX IT! RIGHT?
UH-- RIGHT!
HOURS LATER...
THERE SHE IS, LI'L BRITCHES-- YIRJOSHINMEE!
HALF OF IT'S NOTHING BUT WARE-HOUSES!
YOU GOT IT! SINCE THE ISLAND'S NEAR SHIPPING ROUTES, THE NATIVES MAKE A FORTUNE RENTING STORAGE SPACE! PICKER'S WAREHOUSE IS DOWN THERE SOMEPLACE!
SO FAR SO GOOD! NOW LET'S FIND WAREHOUSE SEVEN-TEEN!
HELLO? ANYBODY HOME?
THERE'S GOTTA BE A LIGHT SWITCH IN HERE!
A-HA!

FLICK
THAT'S IT? ONE CRATE?
MAYBE IT'S FULL OF REAL EXPENSIVE GOLD AND JEWELS AND STUFF!
I DON'T CARE IF IT'S FULL O' YESTERDAY'S LAUNDRY! IF PICKER WANTS IT, PICKER'LL GET IT--BEFORE 10:00 A.M. TOMORROW!
C'MON, LET'S LOAD IT UP!

SOON...
WELL, GANG, IT'S ALMOST MIDNIGHT!
LOOKS LIKE BECKY'S GOT NUTHIN' TO WORRY ABOUT-- WE'LL MAKE IT BACK TO CAPE SUZETTE WITH TIME TO SPARE!

TICK! TICK!

TICK! TICK! TICK!

TICK! TICK! TICK!

PLING!

CLICK!

CHIR?
CHIR?
CHIR! CHIR!

CHIR?
CHIR?
CHIR? CHIR?

PRETTY NIGHT, ISN'T IT? THERE'S SOMETHING WONDERFUL ABOUT BEIN' UP HERE WITH THE MOON. KINDA MAGICAL.
YEAH-- I KNOW WHAT YOU MEAN.

HEE HEE HEE!
HEE HEE!

BALOO, WHAT'S THAT OUTSIDE YOUR WINDOW? IT'S SOMETHING BRIGHT!
OOO, COULD BE A FALLIN' STAR, OR A COMET, OR A--

--FIRE!!

HANG ON--I'M TAKIN' HER DOWN!
CLICK!
WILDCAT, GET READY WITH THAT FIRE EXTINGUISHER!
READY, BALOO!

FWAASH!

SPLUSHHH!

Y'KNOW, WILDCAT--IF YOU'DA FIXED THE ENGINE EARLIER LIKE I ASKED YOU TO, THIS WOULDN'T HAVE HAPPENED!
OH, NO WAY, BALOO! THAT ENGINE NEEDED WORK, BUT IT SHOULDN'T HAVE CAUGHT ON FIRE!
LIKE, SOMETHING ELSE MUST'VE HAPPENED!

WELL, LET'S GET TO WORK FIXIN' IT!
WE CAN'T AFFORD TO WASTE ANY TIME!

LATER...
SO HOW'S THE SCHEDULE, LI'L BRITCHES?
WE CAN STILL MAKE IT TO CAPE SUZETTE BEFORE THE DEADLINE-- AS LONG AS NOTHING ELSE GOES WRONG!

ZHH-ZHH!
ZHH-ZHH!

HEY-- WHAT'S GOIN' ON?!

BALOO! THE STARBOARD PONTOON IS COMING OFF!!

NO WAY WE CAN LAND ON IT, BALOO!
BUT IF WE CAN'T LAND, HOW CAN WE FIX IT?!

WE'LL JUST HAVE TO FIX IT ON THE FLY!!

AND SO...
WAY TO GO, WILDCAT! I GUESS THAT *INVENTION* OF YOURS IS MORE *INVENTIVE* THAN YOU *THOUGHT!*
RRRMMMM!
ZZCHKT!
FFZZKT!

SNAP!

LATER...
I FIGURED IT *OUT*, LI'L BRITCHES!
FIGURED OUT *WHAT*, BALOO?
WHAT'S GOIN' *ON!*

THERE'RE *GREMLINS* IN THE PLANE!
?!

HA HA HAAA!
OH, *C'MON*, POPPA BEAR! THERE'S *NO* SUCH THING AS *GREMLINS!* THEY'RE JUST--

--HUH??
TOONK!

NEEERRRRMMM!!
THERE-- I TOLD YA! GREMLINS ARE IN MY PLANE, AN' THEY WANNA KILL US!
BALOO, I DON'T CARE IF IT'S GREMLINS OR NOT! JUST PULL UP!!

Whew!!
OKAY THEN, LI'L SMARTY BRITCHES-- IF GREMLINS DIDN'T DO THAT, THEN WHAT DID?
I DON'T KNOW, BUT--
THOONK!

YIIIEEEE!!
AAAAGH!!
TONK!

REEERRRMM

HEE HEEEE HEE!

OH MAN, NO DOUBT ABOUT IT-- GREMLINS ARE IN MY PLANE! WE'RE DONE FOR! WHY, THE STORIES I'VE HEARD--!
CALM DOWN, POPPA BEAR! GREMLINS ARE NOTHING MORE THAN AVIATION FOLKLORE! SOMEBODY MADE THEM UP, JUST LIKE THE--

--BOGEYMAAAN!!
FWUNK!

HEE HEE HEEE!

BELIEVE ME NOW?
ULP!

HEY, BALOO, I WAS TAKIN' A NAP AND I FELL OUTTA THE BUNK--
--TWICE!
GO BACK TO SLEEP, WILDCAT!
AND STRAP YOURSELF DOWN!

GREMLINS OR NO GREMLINS, WE GOTTA KEEP FLYIN'-- FOR BECKY'S SAKE!
WE CAN'T LET ANYTHING SLOW US DOWN NOW!
STRAP MYSELF DOWN?
WELL... OKAY!

BUT TIME MARCHES ON...
UNTIL...
AW, IT'S NO USE, LI'L BRITCHES--WE'RE NOT GONNA MAKE IT!
LOUIE'S

IT'S 9:55 AN' WE'RE ONLY COMIN' UP ON LOUIE'S NOW!
YOU CAN'T GIVE UP, BALOO! HIGHER FOR HIRE MEANS EVERYTHING TO MIZ CUNNINGHAM!

IT MEANS A LOT TO ME, TOO, KID. BUT WE LOST TOO MUCH TIME TO THOSE GREMLINS.
ALL I WANT NOW IS A GOOD SHOULDER TO CRY ON...

AND SOON, AT LOUIE'S PLACE...
I LOST HIGHER FOR HIRE, LOUIE! BECKY'LL NEVER FORGIVE ME!
THERE THERE, BIG DADDY!

I CAUGHT IT, BALOO! I CAUGHT THE GREMLIN!
SEE??

YOU MEAN TH-THAT'S A G-G-GREMLIN? THAT'S WHAT ALMOST KILLED US LAST NIGHT?!
I GUESS SO! I FOUND IT STUCK LIKE THIS IN MISTER PICKER'S CRATE!
CHIRR!
CHIR! CHIR!

WHOA, CUZ-- THAT'S NO GREMLIN!
IT'S NOT?

EEEK!
SMACK!
THEN WHAT IS IT??

THAT, MY MAN, IS A PIECES MONKEY!
A PIECES MONKEY--?!?
YEAH--AS IN IT TAKES-THINGS-TO-PIECES!!

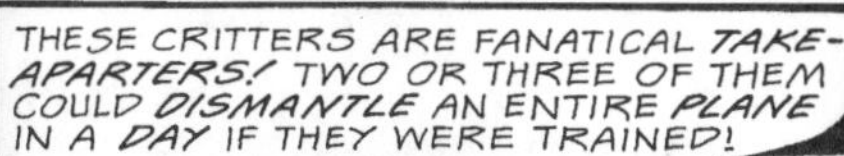
THESE CRITTERS ARE FANATICAL TAKE-APARTERS! TWO OR THREE OF THEM COULD DISMANTLE AN ENTIRE PLANE IN A DAY IF THEY WERE TRAINED!

THEY'RE ILLEGAL TO SELL AS PETS 'CAUSE THEY'RE IMPOSSIBLE TO CONTROL! THEY'RE REAL SMART AND REAL MEAN!
WHERE'D YOU GET ONE, CUZ?
CHIR! CHIRR!

I DIDN'T! I MEAN, I DON'T KNOW WHERE IT--
--WAIT A MINUTE--
BALOO, ARE YOU THINKING WHAT I'M THINKING?
I THINK I AM!

YOWZA-- I THINK I'M THINKIN' WHAT YOU TWO ARE THINKIN'! AND I THINK YOU'RE RIGHT!
I THINK I'M CONFUSED!

DON'T WORRY ABOUT IT, WILDCAT-- JUST SHOW ME EXACTLY WHERE YOU CAUGHT OUR LITTLE FRIEND!
OKAY!

A BUNCH OF OLD SUITS AND HATS?
THIS IS PICKER'S IMPORTANT CARGO?!
COULDA USED A MOTHBALL OR THREE IN HERE!

HEY, BALOO--LOOK AT THIS!
IT'S SOME KIND OF CAGE!

I FOUND THE LITTLE GUY TRYIN' TO PULL THE NAILS OUT OF THE CRATE WITH THE OTHER TWO!
THE OTHER TWO? THE OTHER TWO WHAT?
THE OTHER TWO PIECES MONKEYS!

YOU MEAN THERE'RE MORE OF 'EM? WHY DIDN'T YOU SAY SO?!
NOBODY ASKED!
WHERE ARE THEY? IF THEY GET LOOSE ON MY ISLAND--!!

THERE THEY GO!
YAAAGH!! THEY'LL TEAR MY PLACE APART!!
LOUIE'S
STOP THEM!!

GO TO IT, FELLAS!
I'LL GUARD THE DOOR!

WILDCAT, LOOK OUT--!!
CHIR-CHIR!
BOOMP!

GOTCHA!
OH NOOOO!!
CHIR!
CHIR-CHIR!

SPLORT!!
WHAM!

WELL, I'LL BE A PIECES MONKEY'S UNCLE!
WHAT ARE THEY DOING?

TAKIN' A MUNCHY BREAK, I'D SAY!
NOBODY MOVE! I GOT AN IDEA!
CHOMP! CHOMP!

LOUIE, REAL SLOW NOW-- GET ME ANOTHER JAR OF MARASCHINO CHERRIES! WHATEVER YOU DO, DON'T STARTLE THESE GUYS!
ONE JAR MC'S COMIN' UP!
CHOMP!

HERE, CUZ!
JUST IN TIME!
CHIR-CHIR?

HERE, MONKEY-MONKEYS! C'MON, COME GET THE CHERRIES, YA ROTTEN LITTLE MONSTERS!
CHIR-CHIR!
KIT, BRING THE CAGE OVER HERE! PUT IT ON THE FLOOR!

GET READY TO OPEN THE DOOR!
READY, POPPA BEAR!

FWIP!
CHIR-CHIR!

WELL, HOW DO YOU LIKE THAT? PIECES MONKEYS CAN BE CONTROLLED AFTER ALL!

SOON...
NOW LET ME GET THIS STRAIGHT--
--THAT T. BONE PICKER PERSON SENT YOU ON A WILD GOOSE CHASE AFTER DERELICT CARGO--
--AND THEN DELIBERATELY PUT THESE CRITTERS IN YOUR PLANE SO YOU'D MISS THE DEADLINE, IS THAT IT?

THAT'S HOW IT LOOKS TO ME. I WAS SET UP FROM THE GET-GO.
OH MAN, I CAN'T GO BACK TO HIGHER FOR HIRE AN' FACE BECKY-- I JUST CAN'T!
CUZ, IF THE CONTRACT WAS MADE IN BAD FAITH, IT ISN'T LEGALLY BINDING!

WHAT DIFFERENCE DOES THAT MAKE IF I CAN'T PROVE IT?
I SIGNED THE STUPID THING, DIDN'T I? THAT MAKES IT A LEGAL CONTRACT, PERIOD!!

GEE...WHAT IF WE CONVINCED MISTER PICKER TO RECONSIDER--?

AND SOON, BACK AT THE BUSINESS IN QUESTION...
PLEASE, MISTER PICKER--CAN'T WE WORK THIS OUT SOMEHOW? I'VE INVESTED MY LIFE IN HIGHER FOR HIRE!
I DO SYMPATHIZE WITH YOUR POSITION, MIZ CUNNINGHAM, BUT--
--BUSINESS IS BUSINESS, YOU KNOW!

BOSS-- THE BEAR'S BACK!
AND HE'S GOT A CROWD OF PEOPLE WITH HIM!

BOY, WHAT A JOURNEY! I TELL YA, IT TOOK ME A WHILE TO GATHER EVERYBODY TOGETHER!
BALOO, WHERE HAVE YOU--?!

NOW, BECKY, I KNOW I MISSED THE DEADLINE AN' I'M REAL SORRY 'BOUT THAT, BUT A CONTRACT IS A CONTRACT! SO I FIGURED I'D DO YOU A FAVOR AN' MAKE THIS PAINFUL TRANSACTION NICE AND TIDY, OKAY?
WHAT--?
WHY--?
WHO ARE ALL THESE PEOPLE?!

WHY, THESE ARE ALL OF OUR CREDITORS!
SINCE WE OWE SO MUCH MONEY TO THESE GUYS, I FIGURED MISTER PICKER OUGHTTA GET TO KNOW 'EM RIGHT AWAY, 'CAUSE HE'LL BE DEALIN' WITH 'EM FOR A LOOOONG TIME!
!!

LET'S SEE--WE OWE THE BANK, THE HARDWARE STORE, THE MACHINE SHOP, THE PLUMBER, THE ELECTRICIAN--OH, AND DON'T FORGET THE LANDSCAPER AND THE FURNITURE SUPPLY STORE AND THE BURGER STAND AN'--
PAY UP, MISTER!
YOU OWN THIS PLACE NOW?
YOUR PAYMENTS ARE SIX MONTHS OVER-DUE!
BILL
BILL
BILL

PAY UP! PAY UP!
PAY UP!
WAIT--
--UH, FELLAS, LISTEN TO ME--
--I-I DIDN'T KNOW--!!
BILL
BILL

BOYS, RUN FOR THE PLANE! WE'RE BLOWIN' THIS TOWN!

I... I DON'T UNDER-STAND!
BECKY, MISTER T.BONE PICKER IS NUTHIN' BUT A PENNY-ANTE CROOK WHO HAD A CLEVER IDEA HOW TO HUSTLE HIMSELF A FREE BUSINESS!

SO ME AN' THE BOYS COOKED UP AN IDEA THAT WOULD MAKE OL' PICKY RECONSIDER THE DEAL!
YOU AND WHAT BOYS?
RRRRIP!

US BOYS!
PRETTY CLEVER OF US, HUH?
AN' MISTER PICKER HIM-SELF PROVIDED THESE NIFTY DISGUISES!

BUT YOU JUST LET HIM ESCAPE! IF HE'S A CROOK, WE'VE GOT TO CALL THE POLICE--

NAW, I DON'T THINK THAT'LL BE NECESSARY...

"...IN FACT, I'M SURE OF IT!"
CHIR-CHIR!
CHIR-CHIR!